For Silent Unity

I would like to share this
little bit of Light with you —
as you have shared your
light on deep dark nights
with me.

With Love, Alex

A Matter of Time

A MATTER OF TIME

by

Alexander Michael Giorgio

WAKAN
PRESS

A MATTER OF TIME
© Copyright 1998 by Alexander M. Giorgio

8/01

Published by
Wakan Press
P.O. Box 788
Woodacre, CA 94973

ISBN 0-9647542-2-3

Cover art created by Ken Cruzen
Book designed by Michael Saint James

Gift
author

For Arianna and Daniel

and
the Child
within
every adult

*May the peace of God lighten your steps
and quicken your hearts on the
sacred journey Home*

There Are No Coincidences,
No Chance Occurrences In Life.

This tale has found its way into
your hands *now*—not one year sooner or eight
minutes later. Now, this very instant, you are
on the verge of making a great decision.
A simple choice.

Something within you knows
that it is time for you to begin the short walk
back to the Home you have never left.

The portal is open.

The choice is yours.

AUTHOR'S NOTE

Within this tale are woven the laws of physics, the paradox of illusion and reality, the interrelationship between time and space, perception, the ego, the function of forgiveness, the still, small voice within each of us, and many other concepts born of the dance between our physical and spiritual worlds.

When we look into and through life, not just at it, a whole new reality presents itself to us.

Place the photographs on the flaps of the dust jacket side by side. Hold both pictures at normal reading distance and fix your gaze on an imaginary spot in between them and about three feet behind. Soften your focus. A three-dimensional third image will emerge.

What once appeared flat, will be transformed into a deeper dimension, a new awareness. The image "opens." So it is with life—and this story. Soften your focus and look beyond appearances. A deeper vision awaits.

This
tale is
dedicated
to Myuríta
and the Old Man,
who patiently shared
their story with me,
to the children, who
were curious enough to
keep asking their
questions, to Eleanor
and Bill, who taught me
how to listen
through the silence
and
to the children of time,
who have begun
the short walk Home.

THROUGH THE TEMPLE CAN BE SEEN
A WORLD THAT LIES
BEYOND THE DREAM

A PLACE PAST TIME
AND DIFFERENCES
PAST FAR AND FEW BETWEEN

SOFTLY GAZE
THROUGH WHAT YOU SEE
NEW WORLDS COME INTO VIEW

VISIONS OF REALITY
REMEMBERED
NOW AS NEW

"Do you believe in time?" she asked.

Three days after the earth-splitting eruption of Mt. Chichero in Mexico's Yucatan Peninsula, I met Myuríta.

I recall sitting in the cool recess of an empty Mayan temple in Palanque, watching teams of village workers outside the ancient ruins. They were sweeping and shoveling buckets of soft gray-white volcanic ash into trucks, carting it to who-knows-where. Truck after loaded truck rumbled past, pushing their way through ash-covered streets.

Other villages also were digging through the aftermath of this violent explosion. It had thrown over one million tons of ash and twenty four hours of darkness in every direction.

My mind began to wander after the trucks, wondering how many times in the past this site had slept under a similar blanket of twilight. I wondered about the stories such a place might hold and the wise people who would have told them.

There is a belief in this region: *"When the earth flows like water and the land is blessed with sacred ash, the long darkness shall be followed by the Great Light. It will be a time of new beginning."*

Beliefs are such curious things.

O N E

"Do you believe in time?" I remember the voice asking. Startled, I turned to meet the voice. I met a young women instead. Twig broom in hand, she swept the silence into a neat little pile at my feet.

Draped in bright yellows and blues, she looked at me, or more accurately, *into* me. Ribbons of red were woven into the

blackness of her new-moon colored hair,
framing the timeless curves of her dark
Mayan face. She spoke of truth, wisdom
and beauty, all without a word.

"Do you believe in time?" she asked
again, as if someone were hard of hearing.

I glanced quickly at the door of the
temple to see who she was tossing her
question at, only to see another cloud of
ash dancing behind a truck, coughing its
way down the road.

○

"Believe in time?" I thought to myself,
turning to face her and her question. "What
did she mean *believe* in time? Time is
something that you cook your eggs and miss
your bus by. Time is something that passes
slowly when you want things to hurry up
and rushes by all too fast when you want to
hang on to each and every moment. Good
times. Bad times. Time is something that
just *is*, not something we have an option to
believe in or not.

O

"Of course I believe in time," I
concluded, feeling that unless I answered
yes to her question, she wouldn't let me go.

"Then I have a message for you and the
other children," she said matter-of-factly.

"Children?" I asked. "What children?"

"Look through the opening in the wall
over there," she directed, "through the
portal. There is one now."

Shifting positions, I became aware of an
opening in the wall adjacent to the door. It
stood nearly heart level over the carved
stone floor. Its T-shape resembled the upper
half of a human form, arms outstretched in
an expression of freedom and joy. Beneath
the opening I caught my reflection in a
clear pool of water with only an empty
room behind me. I could see no child.

I began to wonder if the intense tropical
heat was playing with the woman's mind, or
perhaps with my own.

She burst into my thoughts. "Will you do this?" she asked patiently, as if she knew what my answer would be. "You must share the message with the rest of the children. Will you do this?"

I decided to humor her and agreed to her delusion. In the steam bath of an afternoon, I nodded yes.

"Very well," she said. "Then I will share this story with you. It is an ancient message you are now responsible for."

Sensing a rather lengthy tale which undoubtedly would last longer than I would, I searched for an escape clause. "However, there may be a small problem," I lied. "You see, I don't have much time."

"None at all," she smiled. "But you have agreed. Look to your reflection in the pool once again." She motioned with a tilt of her broom handle to the T-shaped opening framing the empty chamber beyond.

Coming up empty-handed in my reach for an excuse, I followed the path of her beckoning broom.

O

I turned to the opening and noticed that
my reflection in the small pool beneath the
portal had become washed out, much like
an overexposed photograph. My reluctant
glance now became a certified stare as I
realized what was happening.

The chamber beyond the portal had
begun to take on a translucent glow. Light
emanating from some point in the chamber
came pouring into the room where I stood.
I squinted, then rubbed my eyes, not sure if
it were my eyes or the scene which was out
of focus.

What felt like eons and an instant, all
folded together, came hurtling through the
deepening portal. The stark, dimly lit room,
sleeping on a gray-white ashen sea, burst
into a dense forest-like environment.

O

I now looked out onto an unfamiliar
land peopled with brilliant emerald trees
and a curious thick scrub thumbing its way

through the thicket. Brightly colored creatures with songs and shapes I didn't recognize, rested on the distant branches.

Central to the foliage was an area which relaxed into a wide expanse of meadow, supporting a sky the color of turquoise reaching for royal blue. It appeared that dawn was approaching, bringing with it a new world, scrubbed clean.

Immense canyon walls embraced this timeless scene, holding it softly as the sound of several waterfalls echoed through an arroyo nearby. A cool, gentle breeze caressed my body. With it came the most beautiful scents imaginable, reminiscent of honeysuckle and jasmine, offered from luminescent flowers growing just beyond the meadow.

O

Within this newly created landscape, individual forms of light began to take shape. They seemed to be that of an old

man and a group of childlike beings
dancing about him. The light forms
solidified into delicate bodies as the
unmistakable laughter of children at play
somersaulted through the air.

Unnoticed, I continued to watch, as the
old man carried himself under a robe of
shimmering colors. The shifting hues
changed size and shape, leaping from
translucent to solid and back again in
perfect rhythm with his gentle movements.

Accompanying this visual feast were the
children, all dressed in cloud tops and
sunsets. They were surrounded by the
sounds of a celestial symphony echoing
their carefree playfulness.

From my fog of amazement and disbelief,
I heard Myuríta's comforting voice. Its
richness and sincerity touched a chord deep
within me, a chord which had lain
dormant, silent, since the days of my own
childhood.

T W O

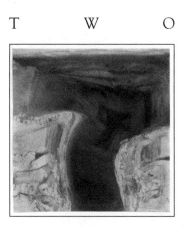

"ONCE UPON A TIME," her voice offered
lovingly from afar, "in a land far, far away,
there was a very old man. He was a wise
and kindly soul with soft chestnut eyes that
would welcome you in, quick as a wink.

"On this particular day, the old man's
great-great-grandchildren were playing
along a fallen log he had chosen for his rest

that morning. Peals of laughter went running after the children as they chased one another 'round and 'round him…"

Myuríta's voice became lost in the portal, as the children and the old man began to speak for themselves.

"Tell us a story, Great-Great-Grand-father!" the children shouted, piling up in a tangle of arms and legs in front of him. "Tell us the story of the children of time!" one squealed. "Please! Please!" the rest chimed in.

"Of course, of course, little ones," he chuckled. "Let's see, where shall I begin?" he wondered aloud.

"Why at the beginning, of course," chided one of the children as she drew herself closer to him.

The old man's robe swirled from the lightest yellow to the deepest green. "Well you see children, that's the problem. This story is so old and happened so long ago, that it begins even before time itself."

The hush of their voices hung in the air as they tried to imagine a time before time.

THREE

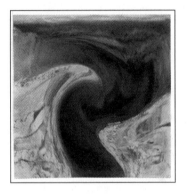

"ONCE UPON A TIME," he began, "even before there was a time to be upon, there was One."

"One what?" they asked.

"Just One." he replied. "There was nothing else because the One was all there was. It was everything and everywhere. It loved all of Itself and knew no separation.

It only knew Love and Joy and Peace
because that's all there was. That's all It
was. It was Love.

"Then for some mysterious and
unexplainable reason, there crept a mad
idea, in which a tiny speck of the One
became all too serious and remembered not
to laugh. It thought it could be separate
from the rest."

"But if the One was all there was," one
child wondered, "how could a part of it be
separate from the rest?"

O

"That's just it," the old man replied with
the lift of an eyebrow. "It couldn't. Being
All, there was nowhere the little part could
go and be separate from the One, but it
thought there was. In fact it was at that
very instant of believing it could be
separate, that all the seriousness and
confusion began."

The children drew themselves even
closer together, their cloud tops bumping

and sunsets shimmering. Even the opalescent scrub surrounding the meadow seemed to inch a breath nearer.

O

"It seems that somehow an **I** had formed," he offered, "which managed to wriggle its way into the timeless Peace. This squeezed **A** completely out of the picture and PEACE became PIECE, an undeniable state of separation.

"Since the separate piece no longer felt it was supported by the One, the little piece decided to create its own supportive framework. That's when time and space and all the physical laws were dreamed up. After all, time and space were non existent, that is until the little piece thought it was separate."

O

"You mean before the separation there wasn't any time *or* space?"

O

"That's right. You see, until that moment, there was no place one was not, and no time in which to get there. But from the separate piece's perception, that was no longer the case.

"Now then, since time and space were born at the same instant, they became inseparable partners. Wherever one would go, the other would follow. If one changed, the other would change right along with it. In fact, they became such close friends that unless you had a special pass between the universes, you had to take time along, to go anywhere."

The celestial music that had been playing with the children softened as one of the cloud tops adjusted herself around the youngest child, who had fallen fast asleep.

"So then the One had to obey the new rules of time and space, too?" one of them asked.

"No, no, my little ones. Only the piece

of the One that thought it was separate
seemed to be trapped in time and space.
After all, it was only the piece that
dreamed up the new laws, which actually
believed in them."

O

"I'll bet the One became very upset with
the piece that thought it was separate. It
probably didn't love that part of itself
anymore," said one of the children, looking
far off across the meadow of what appeared
to be lavender and sage.

"Well, actually, it loved that piece of
itself very much, but you know, the separate
piece did think the One was angry with it.
That belief made the little piece feel guilty
and fearful about becoming separate. In
time, it became very sad and even more
fearful than it already was."

"Did the little piece cry?" asked one of
the boys softly.

"Oh yes, very much so. But it didn't

want the One to see its tears or know it was afraid. So, do you know what that little piece did?" he asked.

"What?" they wondered.

"It built a wall around itself to hide and protect itself from the One."

A shower of rainbows flowed from the openings within the arms of his robe as he gestured to the children.

"But if the little piece was still really a part of the One, how could it hide?"

O

"That's just it," he said. "It couldn't really hide. But it thought it could. Do you remember when you were very young and you wanted to hide from me? You would cover your eyes with your hands and think I couldn't see you."

"I remember!" one of the children exclaimed. "I used to be so surprised you could find me."

"But, of course, I could find you. I

could always see you—whether you could
see me or not. It was like that with the
One. Well, by now, the little piece was
feeling quite ashamed of itself for becoming
separate. So to make the wall it had built
around itself even tougher, the little piece
that thought it was separate became even
more separate within itself.

"It kept dividing and dividing until
anywhere any piece of the separation would
look, all it would see were other separate
pieces. These were the children of time,
and that was just what the little piece
wanted. It thought the One would never
find it in all that mess of separation."

"Like I thought you would never find me
when my eyes were closed," one child
exclaimed.

"Exactly! So the little piece worked out
a bargain with its new friends—time and
space—that as long as they were all
together, the dream of separation would
hold up. They came up with a plan that

combined two ideas of separation. The first part of the plan was the idea of 'me' and 'you.'"

O

"You mean they thought *us* up?"

"Not *us*, but 'me' and 'you.' It was essential to keep reminding the huge numbers of the children of time who were now created, that they were separate. What better way than to have them remind themselves!

"They passed out instruction sheets so each child of time knew it was to call itself 'me' and all the rest of the children of time 'you.'

"Now for the second part of the plan, time and space wanted a message to be sent around. It was to remind the children of time to visit each other as often as they could."

"So they wouldn't be lonely, right?"

"Unfortunately, that's what time and

space wanted the children of time to think.
They knew that as long as there was
somewhere for the little pieces to go, there
was somewhere they were not. This too, of
course, would keep reminding them of their
separateness.

"And as if that weren't enough, time,
space and the little piece began to finalize a
plan which would ensure that the children
of time would never discover their true
Identity and return to the One."

F O U R

THE OLD MAN STOOD UP SLOWLY, stretching
his hands to the heavens. He mirrored the
flaming purple vines that wound
themselves lovingly through the nearby
thicket. The children shifted positions,
rolling over with their backs against the
meadow's soft face. Some stared into the
clouds napping overhead, as they pondered

his story thus far.

"It sounds pretty complicated to me," one child said as she nibbled on a leaf of violet pastille.

"Yes," another added. "It *is* very confusing."

"That's just it, you see," the old man began, as he seated himself on the log again. "Time, space and the separate piece needed to make it quite complicated so they would feel safe. They figured the more confusing things became, the less chance there would be for the children of time to see the dream of separation for the illusion it really was.

"They also thought a general title for their brand new business of separation was in order. The little separate piece chose 'ME' as its symbol of separation. Time, space and all the physical laws which were now made—laws of separation—wanted more of an action word, so they chose 'GO.' The only problem was that they needed a three-letter name for their new venture."

O

"Why did they need a name with three letters?"

"They thought it would show status. After all, the One, the All, even God, were three-letter names, and they wanted one, too. Remember now, they had chosen ME and GO as their names. To combine them into one, and have only three letters, they needed to either drop the M or the O.

"After much deliberation, they decided that MEG just didn't have the drive that EGO would, so they stuck with EGO as the title of their joint venture in separation.

"Now, just to make sure the EGO would stay together, they figured out another clever scheme. As long as the EGO was in the past or future, its separation was insured, for if it ever entered the present, where there was no time, there would be no separation and the EGO would be no more."

O

"I'll bet that once they got the EGO started, they were afraid that if it ever did slip into the present, the little separate pieces would die, right?"

O

"Most certainly. So to make sure that never happened, they gave the EGO the attributes of judgment, expectation and guilt.

"Any one of the three new attributes alone would keep the EGO in the past or future. And since most of the attributes would be working together—well, you can see how it would be quite difficult for the EGO to slip into the present.

"They figured this last scheme was the EGO's *final* *ending* and *attack* on *reality*, so they lumped all its attributes under the general heading of *f.e.a.r.*. EGO, who by now had a mind of its own, thought *f.e.a.r.* had a nice ring to it."

O

A sound like thunder whispered in the distance.

"What would happen to the EGO if it ever *did* enter into the present?" a little one asked.

"It would just dissolve into the nothingness from which it was made."

"And then what would happen?" she persisted.

"Then, my children, those little pieces of separation, the children of time, would realize that they really weren't separate, that in fact, they were very much a loving part of the One and had never ever been separate, but only dreamed for a short time that they were."

"You mean the children of time actually woke up from the dream?" another child asked.

"In a sense, yes, the very moment it began. But for all of them to experience their awakening from the dream, they had to join together in the present."

ALEXANDER MICHAEL GIORGIO

"I don't see how they could do that with
the EGO working against it." said one of
the children, pulling mindlessly at a baobab
root.

O

"That's the trick. They would need to let
go of *f.e.a.r.*, with its judgment,
expectation and guilt."

O

"But how in the world could they do
that?" another asked, with a small shard of
hopelessness caught in his throat.

"With forgiveness," he answered.
"Forgiveness was the key that unlocked the
door to the present."

"You mean whenever one separate piece
would forgive another piece for doing
something wrong in the first place?"

"No. That type of forgiveness just took a
past event and made it real. Then, through
guilt, the other piece was forgiven. It was

one of the EGO's most clever tricks.

"You see the EGO was quite sharp. It knew that if the children of time discovered *true* forgiveness, their discovery would shift them out of the past and future and into the present. Of course that would spell an end for the EGO.

"Do you know what the original term for true forgiveness was?" he asked the children.

"No, please tell us Great-Great-Grandfather."

"It was to 'give forth.' But the EGO and its upside-down perception thought it would be smart and reverse the term 'give forth,' which holds no judgment, expectation or guilt, no *f.e.a.r.*, into the more familiar term—forgive. And, as the EGO hoped, forgiveness of another separate piece became hopelessly entwined with judgment, expectation, and, of course, guilt.

"Now true forgiveness, giving forth, meant just what it said, to give forth."

"But what was given?"

O

"Love. Because in reality, outside of the perception of the dream of separation, love was all there was. You see, the love shared when giving forth was unconditional. There was nothing attached or implied. It brought no ultimatum with it. So, by giving forth unconditional love in *every* instance, every single child of time now had the opportunity to find its way back home.

"Seeing as how the EGO had carefully planned everything though, it wasn't as easy as it seemed. Instances of unconditional love were far and few between.

"Alas, I'm afraid that even though the dream of separation, time and space, and the call and subsequent return to Oneness took place long ago, in an instant of an ancient past, the children of time still seemed stuck within the dream.

"They were unable to awaken from their fitful sleep of separation. It seemed the little pieces were now too rooted in the past and future which kept them slaves to time.

"Their only hope of escape lay in the wisp of a crack between the past and future. The door out of the dream was lodged in the present."

○

Quite unexpectedly, an imperceptible zephyr, carrying the sweetest scents of cardamom, elfenberry and vanilla, surprised the children with her presence. For an instant, they became lost in the essence of Love.

"DIDN'T THE ONE GET WORRIED that all this was happening?" a little boy asked, finally answering the tug of concern that had been pulling at his heart.

"No, not worried, for the One knew the little pieces were just dreaming of separation and would wake up in no time."

"When their alarm clock went off?"

"Not quite," the old man said, smiling to himself. "No, as soon as the One knew there was a piece dreaming of separation, the One sent a special messenger into the separate piece's dream to gently awaken the piece and guide it into the present. Once in the present, the little piece, which by now, you remember, had become many separate pieces, would regain its full remembrance of the One."

O

"But what was so special about the messenger?" asked one child whose curiosity came tumbling out.

"The messenger had the unique gift of being able to interact with the children of time in the dream while at the same time knowing that it was one with the All.

"It was known as the Sender of Peace, whose job was to Inspire Remembrance of the Internal Truth, which knows there is no separation. SPIRIT's whole job involved communicating with all the children of time, without actually becoming a part of the dream of separation."

"But if the children of time were so stuck in the dream, how could it lead them home, out of the dream?"

"From SPIRIT's point of view, the task was a simple one. It acted as a beacon on a distant shore for the weary travelers. The warmth and purity of its Light would beckon the sleeping travelers of time to the comfort of a long-forgotten, but familiar land. It was the call out of time to return home to a tranquility, joy and love only dreamt of, but never experienced, in time."

O

"I don't understand, Great-Great-Grandfather. Even if the children of time were able to be led out of the dream, how could they possibly become aware of SPIRIT's Light?"

"Why simply by being still long enough to listen to SPIRIT's guiding voice, and living by their heart of hearts," he answered.

"Is living by your heart of hearts the same as flying by the seat of your pants?" one youngster asked in all seriousness.

The old man let go with laughter that came bubbling up from the child he used to be.

"Well," he said, finishing off the last of a chuckle as one would the last spoonful of dessert, "they are somewhat alike. To live by your heart of hearts, you must give up all *shoulds*, *have-tos*, *suppose-tos*, *can'ts* and all other ideas of limitation. When that happens, we are open to the moment, which is what we do when we are 'flying by the seat of our pants,' as you so aptly described it.

"You might say it's like flying by the seat of our hearts. That is where the home of true forgiveness is found—giving forth,

SPIRIT's voice and unconditional love.

"Now then, where was I?" the old man asked, as he shook out the remaining bits of laughter that had fallen onto his robe.

O

"You were telling us how the children of time could find the Light home."

"Oh yes, thank you." Clearing his throat of a muffled cough, the old man continued.

"So, in living by their heart of hearts— following their *sparkles*, you might say— and doing only that which made them burst out with a joyful, expansive feeling inside the very deepest part of their being—by sharing unconditional love—they began to see SPIRIT's Light and feel the inner peace and gentle guidance its presence brought with it.

"They began to understand that what they, the children of time, were really experiencing was in fact, a dream. It was an illusion and not the reality they had led themselves to believe it was.

"Well, the EGO knew something was up and started to build an even stronger alliance with *f.e.a.r.* and its attributes of expectation, judgment and guilt. But it was too late. Even *f.e.a.r.* couldn't stop the ever-so-small thread of Truth that was beginning to weave itself through all the separate pieces."

The moon began to show itself over crimson canyon walls, as it rose through a sky preparing itself for bed.

EXCHANGING A DEEP SIGH with a new found moment, the old man paused to reflect on the events of the story he had shared with the little ones gathered about.

He thought of the fearful separation experienced by the children of time, the painful hiding and the deep sadness of never knowing their true home. His own sadness began to lighten as he realized that they had never really left home and were beginning to remember that.

A small dewdrop of a tear, glistening in the corner of the old man's eye, slipped gently down the weathered contours of his face.

"Great-Great-Grandfather, did the children of time ever get back home?" one child asked.

"Please tell us, Great-Great-Grandfather!" another chimed in.

The old man unfolded his legs and stretched out his arms wide apart. He gazed for a moment at the rose of their cheeks, and their eyes so new to this life.

"Well, some say they never did find their way back home out of the dream. Others think that it doesn't matter how it ended. It's only a story fit for spry young children too busy laughing and tumbling about to be concerned with the real things of this world."

O

"What about you, Great-Great-Grandfather? What do you think happened?"

O

"Me?" he thought aloud. "Well you know," he paused, "I believe they made it home all right, the very moment they left. It's just taking a while for the message to get around."

"Do you think we'll hear about the message, Great-Great-Grand-father?"

"No doubt, children," he said. "No doubt. It's only a matter of time."

O

The twilight, which had quietly folded itself around the small group, began to deepen. A second moon, as blue as a tropical sea, was now beginning to rise.

"Come children, it's getting late. It's time we started back."

One by one they rose to their feet.
Clasping hands and locking arms, they
began the short walk Home.

S E V E N

THE SCENE WITHIN the chamber became
hazy, then faded as the old man and the
children began their journey Home. They
left me with the feeling that they had only
begun to share their journey with me.
There was much I had yet to learn.

Once again I was looking through the
T-shaped portal into a darkened room.

Finding the chamber allowed me to find my senses. I whirled around to where Myuríta stood, my eyes drinking in the other side of an empty room. No young woman, just a twig broom leaning against the wall and a message fingered onto the ash covered floor of the temple.

"Please share what you have seen with the children. Perhaps they will remember. With love and joy from the 'seat' of my heart, Myuríta."

E I G H T

OUTSIDE THE TEMPLE, I WAS faced with an ash-strewn street where villagers were sweeping and shoveling up the dusk.

Inside, I was only beginning to understand the message Myuríta had now made me responsible for.

Making my way slowly down the steep temple steps, past the ashes and the

villagers, past the sweeping and the
shoveling, past the daytime and the dusk, I
passed my Self.

> We were beautiful.
> We were Light.
> We were Love

I was one of those children. And I was
just beginning to remember that.

THE PORTAL
LAY INSIDE
YOUR HEART
THE TRUTH FOR ALL TO SEE

OFFERING
FORGIVENESS
WILL SET YOUR
SPARKLES FREE

EPILOGUE

It would be nearly ten years before I heard from Myuríta again.

Ultimately, the adventures of Myuríta, the old man, and the children, lead us to this one very simple reminder:

Discover the present
by following your
sparkles;

doing only that which is totally joyous to the deepest part of your being in each and every moment.

By following those sparkling, expansive, alive feelings that speak to our heart of hearts, we will open to forgiveness, to unconditional love and to that still small voice within.

I wish you well on your journey, knowing that we are traveling as One. I look forward to meeting you...in the present.

✤

FOR TIME YOU

MADE —

AND TIME YOU CAN

COMMAND.

YOU ARE NO MORE

A SLAVE TO TIME

THAN TO THE

WORLD YOU MADE.

✤

From the text of
A Course in Miracles

CREDITS

Cover art adapted from the painting "Disintegration of Infinity" by Kenneth W. Cruzen.

Ken has been a fine artist and illustrator for over twenty years. He received his degree in art from Colorado Institute of art and also holds a degree in business. Ken has won several national and regional competitors including the Ann Taylor Wildflower competition.

His illustrations have appeared on magazine and video game covers, T-shirts, furniture design and children's books. Ken is represented by the gallery Studio 1818 in Denver, Colorado.

He lives in Littleton, Colorado with his wife Seferina and their two children.

3-D photography by Alex Giorgio.
  Dust jacket flaps: Hohokum ruins, Case
    Grande, Arizona, USA.
  Chapter head pages: Mayan "T"emple opening,
    Yucatan peninsula, Mexico. Image swirled by
    Michael Saint James
  Page 13, 64: Mayan arch, Yucatan peninsula,
    Mexico.

Page 5, 72: A *Prayer of Joining* graphic by Aria

Page 67: The quotation is from A *Course in Miracles* © 1975 Foundation for Inner Peace, and is used by permission.

MAKING CONTACT

Alex Giorgio at
LexGiorgio@aol.com

Wakan Press at P.O. Box 788,
Woodacre, CA 94973

Wakan Community at
http://www.nierica.com

Michael Saint James at
peppermike@earthlink.net

Ken Cruzen at
9497 W. Ontario Dr.
Littleton, CO 01240

You can order additional copies of *A Matter of Time* through your on-line bookseller or directly from Spiritual Foreplay. Please send $16.95 US per book plus $3.00 US shipping. For orders of 3 or more, there is no charge for shipping.

Spiritual Foreplay
P.O. Box 446
West Stockbridge, MA 01266

You may also e-mail your order to Sp4play@aol.com, or by phone at: 1-800 THE BOOK, Internet order division.